ATTACK

OF THE GRIEFERS

ANNA KOPP

ISBN: 1534712380
ISBN-13: 978-1534712386

CONTENTS

Chapter 1:   A Catty Conundrum   1

Chapter 2:   A Slimy Situation   5

Chapter 3:   A Weird Wake-up Call   13

Chapter 4:   A Soluble Solution   19

Chapter 5:   The Path to Fame   25

Chapter 6:   Picture Not-so-Perfect   31

Chapter 7:   A Rowdy Reunion   39

Chapter 8:   A Blast from the Past   45

Chapter 9:   A Creepy Crime   53

Chapter 10:   A Bone to Pick   59

Chapter 11:   Hacker the Man   67

Chapter 12:   Never Nether   77

Chapter 13:   A Snowy Surprise   85

Chapter 14:   A Sticky Swamp   91

Chapter 15:   A Tricky Trap   97

Chapter 16:   The Mushroom Meeting   105

Chapter 17:   Avoiding the Void   113

Chapter 18:   A Valiant Victory   117

Chapter 19:   A Final Mission   125

CHAPTER 1: A CATTY CONUNDRUM

Meow!

Red looked up at the sky. It's not where one usually looks upon hearing a 'meow' but these were extenuating circumstances.

It was raining ocelots.

Meow! Meow! Meow!

A baby ocelot landed right on top of his head. Red jumped and it skittered away. What in the world was going on? It rained a lot in the jungle, but it never rained cats. That's just crazy.

The ground was quickly becoming covered with the yellow beasts. Red decided he needed to get somewhere quiet so he could think. He ran straight for his jungle temple house. It wasn't far – he was just out collecting some wood. Everywhere he looked, there were ocelots. The meowing was getting so loud, he had to cover his ears. At last he saw the stone bridge that led into the temple. He hurried across, gawking at the sea of swimming cats in his moat.

Meow!

An ocelot jumped right in front of him! Red tried to stop, but it was too late. He slipped on the stone and fell right into the water. Wipe out! Cats began to swarm him, and for a moment he thought he would drown. But Red wasn't about to let a few felines get the best of him. He pushed them off and climbed back onto shore. Trying again, more careful this time, Red made it to his house and slammed the door behind him.

A sigh of relief escaped his lungs. He could still hear the ocelots outside, their mews muffled behind the thick walls. He changed out of his wet clothes and sat down to think while eating a melon.

Red had seen some strange stuff during his adventures. He got trapped in a Tutorial biome that was impossible to complete. He watched bedrock turn into dirt and diamond swords transform into stinky fish right before his eyes.

But he had never seen it rain anything other than water.

His first thought was that it must have been the work of the Glitcher, or Gil as Red knew him. It was Gil who did all the other stuff by hacking into the root code of the world. However, the Glitcher was now Red's friend, and he vowed to only use his powers for good. Did Gil somehow turn into a griefer again? Or did someone else take up the mantle? Red had no idea, but he knew how to find out. He had to go see Gil.

Red packed all the essentials. Weapons, armor, potions, and food. Who knew what kind of trouble Gil had gotten into? Red hoped he wouldn't have to fight his friend, but the raining ocelots nonsense had to be stopped. And if it wasn't Gil, maybe he could help fix whatever it was that made it that way.

Ready to go, Red looked outside his window. The 'rain' had finally stopped, but the ground was littered with ocelots. Good thing it didn't rain spiders or creepers, he thought. Now *that* would have been bad. He carefully opened the door and began to walk down the bridge. Cats jumped out of his way, splashing into more cats and causing a swirl of black spotted yellow creatures. Red focused on the road ahead. He had to get to Gil as soon as possible, before anything else happened.

But his hopes were slashed when he heard the distant roar of thunder right as he left the jungle and crossed over into the plains. He looked up and gasped. A dark cloud was quickly making its way towards him, and this time it wasn't ocelots dropping down from the sky – it was slimes.

CHAPTER 2: A SLIMY SITUATION

P<small>LOP.</small>

Red ran as fast as he could as the slimes began to drop down behind him.

PLOP. PLOP. PLOP.

Some of the green glops broke into chunks as they hit the ground, making even more mobs. Red wished he could climb a tree or hide in a cave, but the plains were barren of everything except grass. He did see a small pool of water to his left, but since slimes could swim, there was no point in going for it.

The slimes multiplied fast. Red had to get to cover. He knew there was a village just a little bit further and used all his remaining energy to try and make it there.

SQUISH.

A tiny slime fell before him and he stepped in it, covering his foot with the green goo and sticking it to the ground.

"Gross!" Red cried out while shaking off the gunk. He didn't have much time – slimes were beginning to surround him. He quickly put on his armor and took out his diamond sword. If it's a fight they wanted, it's a fight they'd get.

A big slime jumped at him and Red slashed it with his blue blade. It got knocked back, but not for long. Red kept swinging, landing blows on mob after mob. The slimes flew back, but for each one destroyed, another took its place. Red knew his only option was to run, since even someone as strong and experienced as him couldn't take on hundreds of mobs. His foot was unstuck again so he downed a Potion of Swiftness and sprinted away. The slimes followed, but they had no chance. Red ran all the way to the village and knocked on the door of the closest house.

"Please!" he yelled, trying to catch his breath. "Let me in! It's raining slimes out here!"

He immediately realized how silly that sounded, and was about to say something else, when the door opened and a confused villager looked him over. "Raining slimes, you say?"

Red dashed inside and shut the door behind him. He slid down to the floor, tiredness overtaking him. The villager offered some mushroom stew and listened while Red explained everything that happened to him that day.

"Oh my," the villager said once Red's story was over. "I think I'll stay inside for a while until all this blows over."

"That's probably a good idea," Red agreed.

They heard a commotion outside and looked out of the windows. Iron golems were fighting the slimes, smashing them with their giant feet. There was goo everywhere! Luckily, it had stopped raining and once the last slime was taken care of, Red stood up and thanked the villager for his hospitality.

"Good luck on getting to your friend," the villager told him. Red nodded and headed back outside, but stopped in his tracks. With all his detours, he lost track of time and the sky was beginning to darken. For a moment he thought it might be better to stay the night in the village. Who knew what kind of chaos could happen on such a crazy day? But Red knew he needed to get to Gil as soon as possible, and the forest biome where Gil lived was only a little bit further.

Red decided he would try to make it, no matter what. He took a deep breath and began to walk towards the glistening river in front of him, behind which he could see towering trees.

The sun was setting quickly, and soon the light level was low enough to start spawning mobs. Red carefully crossed the river and entered the forest. The leafy tree tops blocked the last of the sunlight, leaving Red to rely on a torch he brought with him. He didn't expect it to be so dark, but now he had no choice. He had to keep going.

A skittering above him made Red freeze. He looked up and searched for the source of the sound. A pair of glowing red eyes descended straight down on top of him! Red fell back and slashed at the spider, injuring it. The spider hissed and attacked again, but this time Red was ready. He destroyed the hairy creature and collected the items it dropped.

Hoping to avoid more spiders, Red sprinted through the trees. Shortly, he saw some torches in the distance, which could only mean one thing – the village! Red ran even faster, using up all his energy.

BUUUUH.

A zombie was somewhere nearby! Red didn't stop to see where. If he hesitated, even for a moment, he could be swarmed with mobs.

The trees finally parted and Red came to a small clearing. He could see the village surrounded by a fence and wandering iron golems. Except in between him and the fence was an entire horde of zombies! Not one, not two, not even ten. Red guessed at least a hundred! He knew zombies spawned in groups, but this was just ridiculous. There was no way he could make it through. Unless…

Red took out his trusty pickaxe and began to dig. He mined just a few blocks down and then straight towards the village. He used his torch to light the way, adding some to the walls as he progressed through the tunnel. He only hoped the zombies didn't hear him.

His hopes were slashed when he heard the familiar low growl behind him.

BUUH.

Red mined faster, hoping he would reach his destination before the zombies got to him. From his calculations, he should be coming up to a basement soon. He knew that because he helped build it for his friend.

BUUUUH.

The sound was coming closer. It echoed in the walls with numerous voices. The zombies have found the underground entrance and were now filing inside! Red's heart raced as he dug, looking over his shoulder for the mobs.

And then he saw them. Green rotting bodies pushing their way through the narrow tunnel with only one goal in mind – get Red. Unsure of how far he had left to go, Red decided he had to stop the zombies from getting further under the village. He stopped and began to put up a wall of dirt behind him, cutting the zombies off – and trapping himself. With air quickly running out, he made a stairwell and with one last swing, he saw the inside of a house.

Red peeked out from the floor and saw a bewildered face staring down at him.

"Red?"

CHAPTER 3: A WEIRD WAKE-UP CALL

"What are you doing here?" Gil asked in surprise. He was sitting up on his bed, staring at the hole Red made in his floor.

"Hey there, Gil," Red said. "I think we may have a problem."

Confused, Gil helped Red out and fixed his carpet. They went into the kitchen and got some food before Red told his friend what was going

13

on. Buddy the cat perched himself next to him, happy to see Red again. Gil listened carefully, and by the end looked both shocked and upset.

"So you thought it was *me* who was doing all this?" he asked Red with a wounded tone.

"At first, yes," Red confessed, "but when I saw the hostile mobs drop down from the sky I knew it couldn't have been. You've done some pranks, but you never meant to hurt anyone."

Gil nodded in relief.

"Is there anything you can do to stop whatever is going on?" Red asked.

Gil shook his head no. "Not without finding out who is doing it. My powers can only fix a problem, not prevent it, and only if I know where and when it's happening. There are millions of lines of code, and I have no way to sort through it all or I would find this griefer myself."

"Do you have any idea who it could be?"

Gil thought about Red's question. He used to know lots of griefers back when he was the Glitcher, and was even on the Griefer Hall of Fame. "Well, it's obviously someone who found a back door in the code the same way I did, except he's not being so nice about it."

14

"That's for sure," Red agreed. "We have to find this griefer and stop him, once and for all."

"But how?" asked Gil. "He could be *anyone*."

"I have an idea," Red said. "Your picture was on the Griefer Hall of Fame, right?" Gil nodded in response. "So that means there's a good chance that this new griefer is on it too."

A smile began to spread across Gil's face. "That's right!"

"Once we know who he is, we can find him," Red continued.

"And I can close the breach so he can't use it again!" Gil exclaimed.

Red nodded. "If it's anything like the one in your house, that means the griefer has to stay in one place in order to use it so we don't have to worry about him running. Our biggest challenge is going to be actually getting to him. His powers are nothing like I've ever seen."

"We're going to need some help," said Gil. "And I know just who to call!"

Red knew exactly who Gil was talking about. He couldn't wait to see his old friends Roxy, Allie, Hunter, and Chase. He usually went on adventures alone, but meeting them made him realize that sometimes, it's better to be with friends.

"Morning is soon," Red said while looking out the window. "We can head to the desert biome as soon as the sun comes up and fries all those zombies outside."

Gil huffed. "Did you forget? I used to be the Glitcher! We don't have to go anywhere to talk to them."

Red raised an eyebrow. "What do you mean?"

"Follow me," Gil beckoned with a grin. He stood up and went to the stairwell that led into his basement. Red curiously followed. He watched Gil push a lever that unlocked a heavy stone door in front of them and entered a small room. It was empty except for one wooden chest in the center. Looking around, Red got even more confused.

Gil walked over to the chest and opened it, motioning for Red to look inside. Red did, and the moment he saw what was in it, he gasped and backed away. There was no treasure or any kind of items, only an endless black hole that led…who knows where.

"What is it?" Red asked, trying not to show his alarm.

"It's the breach," answered Gil. "That's the back door I've been using to alter the code."

Red looked back over to the chest in both awe and unease. "But...how?"

Gil laughed at Red's reaction. "Well, the first time I found it, I just put my head in to see where it went. Once I realized that I could see the entire world's code from within, I've just been jumping in."

Red grimaced at the idea. He remembered Gil as a boy who was too afraid to pick up a sword, but apparently he wasn't as cowardly as Red initially thought.

"You have some guts, Gil," Red confessed, "because there is no way I'd ever be going inside *that*." He pointed at the chest. "Give me skeletons and zombies over bottomless black pits any day."

Gil felt pride filling him. Red, the greatest adventurer he knew, was complementing his bravery! He couldn't be happier.

"Don't worry," he said, "you don't have to go in."

A look of relief washed over Red's face. Gil smiled at his friend reassuringly. "I'll be back before you know it."

Red nervously nodded and watched as his friend jumped in the chest and disappeared into the inky darkness.

CHAPTER 4: A SOLUBLE SOLUTION

"AAAAH!" Allie screamed as a blaze shot another fireball. She jumped out of the way just in time and fired her enchanted bow. The blaze's health dipped, angering it. Three more fireballs came at her, and she prepared for the worst. Luckily, Hunter and Chase ran up and blocked them, sending them back at the blaze.

"Thanks!" Allie told them. She was breathing heavily from all the dodging and fighting. This was the third blaze they've destroyed – and more were coming!

"What in the world is going on?" moaned Hunter. "We can't keep this up for long! Where in the blazes are all these things coming from?"

"I think the real question is *what are they doing in the Overworld?*" said Chase. "Blazes only spawn in the Nether."

"If I didn't know any better, I'd say it was the work of the Glitcher," Hunter told him.

"But we *do* know better," said Roxy, aiming her arrow up in the sky. "And we could really use Gil's help right about now."

More fireballs rained down on them, and the gang fought hard to keep them from setting the entire village on fire. Their house was already burning from the blaze's attacks, but at least they could prevent the same fate from happening to the others.

Hunter looked over at the desert's horizon. "The sun is coming up," he pointed out as he deflected a fireball.

"Maybe the blazes will go away or destroy in daylight," Allie chimed in. "At least I hope so. I have no idea what happens to a blaze during the day because it's never happened before!"

Chase shook his head. "I wouldn't count on it. They're immune to fire so they're probably immune to daylight too."

"Drat," Hunter cursed. The sky was brightening, but the number of blazes was also increasing. If something didn't change quickly, the village was lost.

Roxy closed her eyes and yelled at the top of her lungs. "GIL! HELP!"

Moments passed and nothing happened.

She sighed. "I guess we're on our own."

But then…

CRACK!

"What was that?" cried Allie.

A grin spread over Hunter's face. "It's thunder!"

Allie's eyes widened as she turned up to the sky. A dark cloud appeared out of nowhere, and suddenly water began to pour down over the village, stifling the raging fires. The blazes began to hiss and smoke as the raindrops hit them, until they were put out and destroyed.

The gang cheered and high fived each other. They were saved!

"I have *never* been so happy to get wet," said Hunter.

"Do you think it was a coincidence, or was it really Gil?" asked Allie.

"It *had* to be Gil," said Roxy. She looked up and yelled out, "Thank you!" into the rain.

"I think you're right," Chase agreed. "Come here and take a look at this."

Curious as to what he found, the others huddled around Chase. In front of him was a wooden sign, and on it read, "YW. Meet at the GHoF. – Gil".

"It's a message from Gil!" exclaimed Roxy. "I knew it!"

"What does it mean?" asked Allie.

"Well, the YW stands for 'you're welcome'," explained Chase. "I'm not sure about the GHoF, though."

"The Griefer Hall of Fame," said Hunter in a low voice.

"Why does he want to meet there?" wondered Roxy.

"I don't know, but I don't like it. We're not griefers so they won't even let us in."

"Maybe he knows something about all this craziness that's been going on," said Chase. "I say we go."

Roxy nodded. "I agree."

"Me too," added Allie.

"Alright," said Hunter. "Let's pack up. We've got a long way to go."

"You know where it is?" asked Roxy.

"I sure do, and you won't like it."

CHAPTER 5: THE PATH TO FAME

"I still can't believe you were able to save their entire village *and* get a message to them all from that black hole," said an impressed Red as he and Gil walked down a forest path.

Gil flushed. "It wasn't that difficult. I just-"

"Hold it." Red stopped in his tracks. A rattling sound made him wary.

THUNK!

An arrow lodged itself in his armor!

"Red!" cried Gil. He drew his diamond sword and began to scan the woods for the assailant. Once he spotted the skeleton, he ran up to it and quickly defeated it with his weapon. By the time he got back, Red was already healed and ready to continue.

"Tell me again why you can't just watch over me from the breach while I go to the Griefer Hall of Fame?"

"Because they won't let you in," explained Gil. "It's for griefers only to prevent anyone from hunting them down or reporting them to the mods."

"I guess that makes sense," Red conceded. "How does the whole 'hall of fame' thing work, anyway?"

"Well, once a griefer is recognized by his misdeeds, the information gets sent over to the Hall of Fame. They put up a plaque and photo, and send out an exclusive invitation to the griefer."

"But you're not a griefer anymore."

"No," Gil agreed, "but it's a lifetime membership. The only way to get banned is if you're doing...well, what *we're* about to."

"Oh," Red said quietly. He realized that Gil wasn't just helping him stop this griefer. He was sacrificing his only way into the Griefer Hall of Fame to do it.

"You don't have to do this," he told his friend.

Gil shrugged. "It's ok. I don't want my picture up there anymore anyway. Griefing is a part of my life I'd like to forget."

Red didn't fully believe him, but he decided not to push. They reached the edge of the forest biome, which was coincidentally a beach. All Red could see ahead was water.

"Where to now?" he asked.

Gil gestured to the open ocean. Red nodded and began to craft a boat. They had some lunch and got ready to head out. Gil climbed in the boat first so he could steer it in the right direction, and Red climbed in after him. Taking one last look on land, the boat pushed off.

Soon, Red couldn't see any land at all. The sun was high up in the sky, but he had no idea how far they had left to go.

"Do you think we'll get to the Hall of Fame before nightfall?" he asked Gil.

"We should, but anything can happen these days."

Red tried to take his mind off the endless expanse and looked down into the water. He gasped. Under them wasn't just an ocean – there was a giant stone structure!

"Gil! There's an ocean monument below us!" Red exclaimed.

Gil looked over and his eyes widened. "Wow! I've never seen it before! How cool!"

Red *really* wanted to check it out, but he knew they had no time to stop.

Suddenly, he felt something hit the boat from the bottom. The vessel rocked and Gil almost lost an oar.

"What was *that*?" Gil cried out as Red searched the blue depths for the culprit.

"It's just a guardian," he told Gil when he spotted the blue fish. "There must have been one too close to us from the temple so it aggroed."

Red drew back his bowstring and fired at the guardian. The arrow was slowed down by the water, but it still hit the intended target. The fish was hurt, and its eye began to glow right before it unleashed a beam laser attack! Red ducked down into the boat and once it was safe, he rose and fired again, destroying the guardian once and for all.

Gil sagged in relief. "That was scary."

"We're not out of the woods yet," Red warned.

Gil looked over into the water and froze in fear. An entire school of fish was heading towards them! If they got close enough, they could beam the boat into oblivion!

"We have to get as far away from the temple as possible," urged Red. He wished he could help Gil row, but it just wasn't possible. Instead, he shot as many arrows as he could into the sea of mobs.

"Here, take this!" Red handed over a Potion of Swiftness.

"Will it even work for rowing?" asked Gil.

"I have no idea, but we have to try."

Gil downed the potion, feeling speed coursing through his veins. With renewed energy, he rowed as fast as he could.

"We're losing them!" Red cheered.

One by one, the guardians began to turn around and go back to the temple. Finally, the friends were safe.

Red plopped down on the boat and took a couple deep breaths. "That could have ended *very* badly."

"True," said Gil, "but one good thing came out of us going so fast. We're here!"

CHAPTER 6: PICTURE NOT-SO-PERFECT

Red sprung up and looked in the direction they were heading. His eyes widened in surprise.

"Wow" was all he could say. In front of them was the rare and elusive mesa biome. It was a pretty small island, but the entire ground was crimson colored with red sand and hardened clay. A giant castle stood at the center, tall pillars of stained clay gleaming in the sunlight. It was the most impressive structure Red had ever seen.

They came to shore and after exiting the boat headed toward the castle. As they neared it, Red saw that it was surrounded by a moat. Except the moat wasn't full of water – it was full of lava. A narrow bridge led to the giant double doors that seemed to be the only entrance. Two people in diamond armor stood guard in front of them, no doubt making sure only griefers went through.

Red began to feel a little nervous. What if he wasn't allowed in? What if Gil was mistaken and they *did* revoke his membership? But Gil seemed confident as they walked down the bridge and toward the guards.

Once they reached the doors, the guard on the left gave Gil a welcoming smile.

"Hey there, Glitcher. Long time no see."

Gil smiled back and waved hello to both of the guards. "Hey Max. Hey Kyle. How's it going?"

"Good," said Kyle, the guard on the right. "Who's this?"

Red stiffened, unsure of what Gil would say.

"Oh, that's my friend Red. He's a griefer-in-the-making," Gil lied. "I just brought him here to show him what he should be striving for."

Kyle looked over at Max, who shrugged. "Alright. Have fun!"

Red let out the breath he was holding as the guards let them through and closed the doors behind them.

Red was unable to take his eyes off his surroundings. The castle's interior was even more amazing than the outside. They were in a large hallway, lined with pillars of end stone. The floor shined green with emerald blocks. Even the ceiling was awesome – it was made of glass!

They walked down the corridor and Red noticed pictures on each of the pillars, with descriptions under them. There must have been hundreds!

"Are these all griefers?" he asked Gil in astonishment.

"The ones in this room are the griefers who aren't in this world anymore. They've either been banned or left to another server," Gil replied, settling Red's concerns.

At the end of the hallway was an entrance to another room, but before they left, Red noticed two familiar faces on the wall named Righty and Lefty. They were the griefers who tried to trap him and his friends in bedrock in the Tutorial biome! Gil said they overloaded by adding too much power to their swords and were sent to another world. Good riddance, Red thought, and stepped over through the doorway.

If he thought the last place was cool, this one took the cake. It was a huge dome, constructed completely with diamond blocks. There were a lot less pictures on the walls here, but they were much larger in size – more like the canvas Red had at his house.

"These are the active griefers in this world," Gil explained. Red began to look through the photos to see if he could find anyone who could be capable of the mischief that's been happening.

The first picture had a guy with a huge grin on his face and a block of lit TNT in his hands. His name was 'Blaster'. Apparently, he liked to blow things up.

"Blaster *loves* TNT," Gil told Red. "He blows up *everything*. He'd even blown up *himself* by accident. I doubt he's the culprit."

Red nodded and moved on. The next photo was of a girl in enchanted pink armor with pink hair. Her name was 'Swiper'.

"Swiper can steal anything from right under your nose," Gil said. "She's a master of disguise. She likes to gain your trust and then take everything you own while you sleep."

Red shook his head. "And you were *friends* with these people?"

Gil looked down at the floor in shame. "We weren't *exactly* friends, but I was accepted here. It made me feel like I mattered."

"Everyone matters," Red reassured him. "Let's keep going."

Gil nodded and they went over to the next picture. It was a boy with bright orange hair named 'Multi the Multiplier'.

"I haven't seen him before," said Gil.

"Hmmm, it looks like he takes things and multiplies them somehow. I think we may have found our griefer."

Gil thought about it. "Maybe. It doesn't explain how he made it rain ocelots or slimes, but it does explain the horde of zombies and guardians. We should definitely keep him in mind."

Red agreed and they went on. There were all kinds of griefers, but they kept watch for ones that fit the criteria. Gil found Modder, a guy who made crazy mods, and Red found Hacker, a serial hacker. They both could be responsible for what has been going on.

Seeing the next picture, Red stopped short. It was Gil! The plaque read "The Glitcher", but that's not what Red was worried about. A red X was painted across the photo. Someone knew that Gil had turned good.

"The person who did this has to be our glitcher," Red said.

"But why?" asked Gil.

"Maybe he wants your title," Red guessed.

Gil frowned. "Well he can have it." He walked up to the ruined photo and with one hit destroyed it. "No more Glitcher for me."

Red watched him with wide eyes. Gil really meant what he said about not wanting to be associated with griefing anymore. He was about to ask Gil if he was ready to continue when his gaze set upon the huge picture on the far wall. He thought it was just a painting at first, but now that they were close enough he could tell who was on it.

"Why is there a picture of Herobrine here?" Red asked in confusion. "He's not real."

Gil shuffled sheepishly. "Maybe. Maybe not. The griefers who made this place decided it would be in everyone's best interest to have him on here. You know, just in case he does exist and won't get mad for being left out."

Red shuddered at the thought. "I guess."

"It's safer that way," Gil added. "We all know what Herobrine can do."

"But those are just rumors," Red tried to reason.

Gil shrugged. "Better safe than sorry."

Red wasn't sure he agreed, but he didn't keep arguing. After taking one last look at the empty-eyed photo, he turned around and continued on. Once done, a list of possible griefers in hand, Red and Gil walked out of the castle and waved goodbye to the guards as they crossed the bridge. Max and Kyle waved back and told them to have fun griefing.

"So what now?" asked Red when they were back on the crimson ground. The sun was setting and they needed to get cover quick. "Should we stay the night at the castle?"

Gil grinned. "Follow me!"

Intrigued, Red followed Gil around the lava moat until he saw what was behind the castle – and it took his breath away.

CHAPTER 7: A ROWDY REUNION

Lining the lava moat was the coolest town Red had ever seen. Every building was a perfect square, decorated with all kinds of colored clay: white, red, orange, brown, you name it! Compared to Red's dreary jungle temple, this was a feast for the eyes! There was also a fence with torches surrounding the place. Red and Gil walked up to the gate and Red read the sign in front of it.

"Griefer Town – enter at your own risk." Oh boy, he thought. That's not good.

"Don't worry," Gil assured him, "they don't usually grief on their own kind."

"*Usually*?" Red asked. "That doesn't make me feel much better."

Gil only laughed and went through the gate. The sun was almost gone, and they hurried to the closest inn. There was a person inside, but he looked a bit strange. He wore a black hooded robe and sunglasses.

"Why would he wear sunglasses at night?" Red whispered to Gil.

Gil shrugged. "It's probably best not to ask any questions," he whispered back. He took out a few emeralds and handed them over. "Two beds please."

The villager took the emeralds and pointed upstairs. The friends found their room and collapsed on the comfy beds. After such an exhausting day of traveling, sleep was the only thing on their mind. The world faded to black until...

"Red! Gil! Wake up!"

Familiar frantic screams jerked the duo out of their slumber.

"Wha...what's going on?" asked a sleepy Gil.

"I'll tell you what's going on!" yelled out Roxy. "You're taking a nap while *we're* getting swarmed by mobs!"

Now that got his attention! Red was already up and using his diamond sword to slash away at a giant black spider. Another jumped right on Gil's bed, and he kicked it right between the eyes. The spider flew back and hissed in rage as it hit the wall. Gil grabbed his own sword and raised it just fast enough at the leaping arachnid, destroying it.

The three friends dashed downstairs to find the rest of the gang – Hunter, Chase, and Allie, fighting even more spiders. The inn's owner was nowhere to be seen. Gil and Red joined the fight, and soon the spiders were all destroyed. The friends cheered and high fived each other. Allie and Roxy gave Red and Gil a hug.

"It's great to see you guys again," Allie said.

"You too," replied Red.

Gil smiled. "I see you got my message."

"Of course we did!" exclaimed Roxy. "We just got here, but when we tried to get a room, we couldn't find anyone."

"Until, that is, we went upstairs and caught someone trying to steal all your stuff while you were sleeping!" said Hunter.

"What?" Red and Gil cried out at the same time.

"We stopped him, of course," Hunter bragged, "but when we chased the griefer outside, we got attacked by the swarm of spiders and he got away."

"What did he look like?" asked Red.

"He had on a black robe and sunglasses," Roxy described. Red and Gil exchanged surprised glances. It was the same person they paid for their room!

"But," added Allie, "When he was running away, I could have sworn I saw his hood fall off and reveal pink hair underneath."

"Hmm," Red thought, "a thief with pink hair." He turned to Gil. "Sound familiar?"

"Sounds like Swiper," Gil admitted. "I can't believe I didn't recognize her!"

"It's ok," Red told him. "She had on a great disguise. Even I didn't realize she was a girl."

"Wait, you know this person?" asked Hunter.

"Kind of but not really," Gil tried to explain.

"Do you think she's the one who made all the spiders appear?" interrupted Roxy.

"And the ghasts at our house?" added Chase.

Gil felt bombarded by their questions. "I don't know," he told them. "I didn't think she was capable of something like that, but now I have no idea!"

Red put his hand on Gil's shoulder. "It's ok, Gil. We'll figure it out." He turned to the rest of the gang. "How about we get some sleep and tackle this in the morning?"

"I'll stand watch," Hunter volunteered. "I'm way too pumped up from the fight to sleep."

Red nodded. "That's a good idea."

They headed back to the inn and Hunter stayed downstairs while the others went up and laid on the beds. Red couldn't stop thinking about what they would do in the morning, but tiredness finally won and he drifted off. There were no more surprises that night and they slept peacefully.

Until morning, that is.

CHAPTER 8: A BLAST FROM THE PAST

"So, what's the plan?" asked Roxy while they were all having breakfast. No one ever came back to the inn so they were the only ones there in the morning.

"Yeah," asked Hunter, gulping down some milk, "why did you have us come out here? You know we can't get into the Hall of Fame."

"That's true," Gil replied, "but you don't need to go in. We were already there, collecting information about all the griefers we think could possibly be the new glitcher."

"A new glitcher?" gaped Allie. "Oh no!"

Red nodded somberly. "I'm afraid it looks like that's the case. Whoever is doing this crazy stuff has the same power as Gil, and he or she has to be stopped."

"Did you get any leads?" asked Chase.

"There are a few," Red replied. "Multiplier, Modder, and Hacker are our top contenders. But I guess we can add Swiper to the list now as well."

"It was a little bit *too* convenient that those spiders came right as she was caught," said Roxy.

Gil shook his head. "I don't know. To get into the code you need a breach, and a breach can only stay in one place. You can't move with it. Believe me, I tried. If she was running, there's no way she could have summoned the spiders."

The others fell silent, thinking of a possible explanation, but came up with nothing.

Suddenly, the door swung open and everyone looked up at the figure that walked inside. It was a boy in a white shirt with a picture of a TNT block on it. Red recognized him from the Hall of Fame. It was Blaster, the one who loved to blow things up. Except on his face was a frown, not a smile like in the picture.

And in his hands was a *real* block of TNT.

Everyone froze.

"Which one of you stole my stuff?" Blaster asked with an angry tone.

The friends looked over at each other. "We didn't steal anything," Red told him.

"It must have been Swiper," said Gil. "She tried to take our stuff while we slept. If it wasn't for our friends, we would have been robbed too."

Blaster narrowed his eyes. "I think you're lying. Swiper knows better than to mess with *me*. I'd blow her to smithereens!" He glanced over at the others. "And since when do you have friends?"

"Look," Red stepped in, "you don't have to believe us, but think about it. You must have noticed something strange going on these past few days. Mobs raining from the sky? Spawning in hordes? Traveling through dimensions? It's been wreaking havoc for everyone. All we're trying to do is find the person responsible."

Blaster shrugged. "That's not *my* problem. I have enough TNT to take out anything coming my way. And plus, I'm not a snitch. We griefers stick together." He looked over at Gil. "Which makes *you* a traitor."

"Uh-oh," said Roxy, "this is not going to end well."

An evil grin spread across Blaster's face. "For me, it will. But you guys are screwed." He lit the TNT in his hands and threw it in the middle of the room.

"RUN!" Hunter shouted. Everyone dashed to the nearest exit. The windows on the sides shattered as the friends made their way out. The moment the inn was empty, it exploded with a giant BOOM!

"Is everyone ok?" yelled Roxy. Allie craned her neck to see the others through the smoke.

"We're good!" replied Red, standing next to Gil.

"Us too," Hunter and Chase sounded off.

"Not for long!" Blaster's voice echoed in their ears. Where was he?

The smoke began to clear and the gang froze in place as they saw what he meant. Surrounding them was an entire field of random TNT blocks all the way to the fence. If Blaster lit any of them, the entire town would be destroyed!

Blaster stood just outside the village, a trail of redstone dust at his feet.

"Let's play a game," Blaster proposed. "It's called the 'Four Second Dash'. I'm going to ignite one of these TNT blocks. You have four seconds to get out of the blast zone."

"That's impossible!" Roxy cried out. "They'll just light the other blocks!"

Blaster grinned. "That's the point!" He laughed maniacally and held up a fire charge. "Peace out!" He activated the redstone and ran.

"Go! Go! Go!" Red yelled. The friends turned the opposite direction of the incoming blast and sprinted as fast as they possibly could.

BOOM!

The redstone dust reached the TNT and the first round of explosions sent a shockwave through the air.

"AAAH!" Allie screamed, but she didn't stop. They had to keep going or they would be caught up in the blast.

BOOM! BOOM!

More explosions shook the ground.

"We're not going to make it!" yelled Roxy.

"Yes we are!" Red told her. "Here!" He threw a potion of speed at her and to the others. They downed the liquid and ran even faster, leaving more and more distance between them and the explosions.

BOOM! BOOM! BOOM!

"Just a little further!" encouraged Red. Everyone got a second wind and rushed past the fence and into safety. Once out of the blast zone, they collapsed on the ground, breathing heavily from exhaustion.

"That was insane!" Hunter said while trying to catch his breath.

"It sure was," agreed Chase.

"How did he have so much TNT?" wondered Red. "It seemed like he was ready for us."

"I don't know," said Gil, "but we shouldn't stick around. I doubt he'll let us off this easy."

The others agreed and they stood up, ready to leave the dangerous island.

"Not so fast." Blaster's voice came out of nowhere. Everyone turned toward the sound and saw the griefer with even *more* TNT! "I'm going to get you if it's the last thing I do!"

"Oh no you don't!" Hunter roared and charged at Blaster.

"Hunter! No!" Roxy cried out, but it was too late. Hunter's sword was inches away from Blaster when an explosion rocked them off their feet.

"Noooo!" Allie screamed.

The smoke parted and the friends saw nothing but a hole where Hunter and Blaster stood just moments before.

"Poor Hunter," moaned Roxy. "We have to go home and get him!"

"We will," Red agreed. "He saved our lives by taking out Blaster. It's the least we can do." He picked up Hunter's dropped inventory and after a rest and a meal, the gang headed to the desert biome to get back their friend.

CHAPTER 9: A CREEPY CRIME

"Hunter!" Roxy threw herself at her friend, hugging him.

Hunter accepted her welcome with a grin. "Took you guys long enough."

"Sorry," said Gil. "This was all my fault. I shouldn't have asked you to go to Griefer Town. I should have known you wouldn't be safe there, even with me around."

"It's ok, Gil," Allie reassured him. "There is no way anyone could have known."

"I guess," he mumbled.

"So, what's the plan?" asked Hunter. "I want to go kick some griefer butt."

"I say we go visit the homes of those we have on the list. One of them has to be our guy," Red proposed.

"Sounds good to me."

"Who should we go for first?" Red asked Gil.

Gil pondered for a moment before answering. "Hacker is the closest. He lives in the taiga biome."

Hunter's eyes lit up. "That's where wolves spawn!"

Red nodded. "That's right."

"I've always wanted to tame one," said Chase.

"Me too," Hunter agreed. "It's decided, then. Onward to the taiga!" He began to walk.

Gil shuffled in place. "Actually, even though it's close by we won't be able to get there and find Hacker before nightfall. We should stay here and go in the morning."

Hunter sagged. "Aaw."

"He's right," Red agreed. "It took us a long time to get here from the mesa biome. There's not much time left before dusk, and these days we don't want to be out and about at night. The last time I tried it, I encountered an entire horde of zombies."

"I'm not afraid of a little zombie chopping action," Hunter argued.

"Maybe not," Roxy said, "but you've already been destroyed once today. Do you really want to make it more than that?"

Hunter rolled his eyes. "Fine, fine. We'll go tomorrow."

The group sighed with relief and made their way inside their home. It was still damaged from the blaze swarm, but the beds were intact and that's all that mattered. The friends laid down and closed their eyes, eager for the night to end so they could continue on their adventure.

BOOM!

The beds shook, sending their occupants to the floor!

"What was that?" cried Roxy. The others quickly got up and grabbed their weapons.

"I can't be Blaster...can it?" Red asked Gil. "How did he find us?"

HISSSS. BOOM!

"I don't think it's Blaster," said Hunter looking out the window. "Unless he can summon a horde of creepers, that is!"

The rest followed his gaze and froze. On the sandy outskirts of the desert village was an endless sea of creepers! At the moment, they were on the opposite side of the fence, filling the moat of water with their green bodies. If they exploded in the water, they wouldn't cause damage, but if an explosion happened near the bridge they would be free to go into the town and destroy everything!

"And I thought Blaster was bad! This is ten times worse!" Hunter exclaimed.

"Try a *hundred*," corrected Chase.

"What are we going to do?" whimpered Allie.

"We have to keep them away from the bridge," advised Red. "Roxy, Allie, get your cats and go to the gate. They will make the creepers back up." The girls nodded and disappeared downstairs. "Hunter and Chase, you need to make sure we have materials in case the bridge is already compromised. Can you get some extra fencing and meet us there?" They also listened and quickly left. Red turned to Gil and drew his sword. "We need to protect the town. Let's go!"

They ran outside and saw that a few lone creepers were already in the village. Red and Gil attacked the closest one with their diamond swords. It began to hiss but they destroyed it before it could explode. Working together, they went through all the creepers they could see, until they finally reached the bridge. Red was right – the creepers did blow it up! Unfortunately, there were just enough blocks left for the mobs in the water to make their way up and into the village. Hunter and Chase were already there, but putting in a new gate was useless – the creepers would just blow it up! Allie and Roxy's cats were keeping the horde at bay, but it wasn't enough. Creepers kept making their way through. The girls were firing arrows while the boys fought, making sure none of the creepers exploded.

"We have to let one blow up," said Red.

"What? Why?" asked Hunter.

"So the blocks near the water disappear and the creepers can't get up here," Red replied.

"That's a great idea!" Roxy agreed.

They waited for another creeper to make its way in and Allie shot it with an arrow. It hissed and began to move towards her.

"Hey! Over here you big green dummy!" yelled out Hunter from the opposite side. The creeper stopped and turned around to face him. "That's right, creeps," Hunter taunted. "Bet you can't get me!" The creeper dashed to him, but the timer was almost done. Just as it reached the edge of the broken bridge, it exploded!

"Great job!" Red praised. The bridge was now completely destroyed, leaving the rest of the creepers swimming around in the moat, unable to get up to the higher ground of the village. The friends cheered and completed the fence with a gate, just in case. They lit a few torches and retreated back home.

"This new glitcher is no match for us," Hunter boasted.

The others just shook their heads and laid down, hoping they could finally get some sleep.

CHAPTER 10: A BONE TO PICK

"I'm pumped! I can't wait to give this griefer a piece of my mind!" said Hunter.

"He might not be our man," warned Red. "We're not going to destroy him for no reason."

"But he's a griefer!"

"And so was Gil," Red reminded him.

Hunter wanted to argue but decided it was useless. Instead, he practiced swinging his sword while the others got ready to go. Everyone except Gil.

"Are you ok, Gil?" asked Roxy. "You seem very quiet this morning."

Gil looked up. "I think it's best if I went home while you guys went to the taiga."

"Why would you do that?" asked Chase. "You're part of the team."

Gil sighed. "I'll be more useful as the Glitcher. How else are we supposed to fight someone with glitching powers?"

"I hate to say it, but Gil may be right," Red contemplated. "We might need him to be able to stop the new glitcher."

"We've been doing just fine so far," Hunter argued. "And if it comes down to it, we know Gil won't hesitate to respawn." He turned to Gil. "Come on, do you really want to sit around at home or do you want to join in on the action?"

Gil gave him a small smile. "I'd like to come."

"Then it's settled. You're coming"

Gil nodded. He was happy to be convinced that he should go with his friends. They finished packing and went over to the broken bridge. Together, they fixed it and left for the taiga.

It wasn't long before the sand turned into grass. Spruce trees and large ferns began to pop up around them, along with random patches of snow.

Allie shivered. "Brrr. It's chilly here." She put on armor to get warm, and the rest followed.

"Compared to your home it definitely is," Red agreed, "but believe me, it can get much, much colder. I've been in biomes where ice spikes rise from the ground and snow covers every surface."

"That sounds horrible," Roxy commented. "I like the heat. That's why we live in the desert."

"Do we know where this Hacker's house is?" asked Chase, looking around at the endless forest.

Gil nodded. "It's in the side of a cliff. I've heard stories about it. A 'you'll know it when you see it' kind of thing."

Chase shrugged. "Alright."

They kept walking, finding nothing but a few brown and black rabbits hopping about.

"Where are all the wolves?" whined Hunter in disappointment.

"Good question," wondered Red. "It shouldn't be this hard to find them."

"Do you think it's because of the hacker?" asked Roxy.

"I have no idea, but-" THWACK. Red's armor got pierced with an arrow!

"Skeleton!" yelled Hunter.

"Where did it come from?" asked Chase. THWACK! Another arrow whizzed through the air and hit him. "On the left! In the spruce trees!" he shouted.

They turned and saw white skeleton bones behind the greenery. Except it wasn't just one skeleton. There was a whole bunch of them – and they were all pointing their arrows at the gang.

"Let's get 'em!" Hunter roared and ran to the mobs. He slashed at their brittle bodies, sending bones flying everywhere. The others joined him, dismantling their attackers until they realized that the skeletons just kept coming.

"How is this possible?" huffed Hunter. "For each one we destroy, two take its place!"

"It has to be the work of the new glitcher," Roxy said as she defeated another skeleton.

"What do we do?" asked Allie, alarm showing in her voice.

"Retreat," proposed Red. "I have some speed potions. We can try to make a run for it."

"Uh-oh," said Chase from behind them, "I don't think that's an option anymore."

They turned around to see that the skeletons were now surrounding them. There was nowhere to run! Their armor and weapons were almost broken. It was hopeless.

GRRRRRR.

A menacing growl broke through the rattling of the skeletons, and the mobs stopped attacking.

"Um...what was *that?*" asked Roxy. She looked scared.

"Oh great," Hunter complained. "Just what we need. More mobs who want to eat us!"

"That's not a zombie," said Red.

"Then what is it?"

Red smiled and pointed in the direction of the growl. "Look for yourself."

Hunter and the others looked over and saw a pack of small grey animals that looked like dogs. They were growling at the skeletons, their eyes glowing red.

"Wolves!" exclaimed Hunter. "Finally!"

The skeletons began to run away, but the wolves chased after them. One by one, they destroyed the skeletons, leaving nothing but bones littering the ground.

"Wow," said Chase, collecting some bones, "wolves are awesome!" He held out a bone for a nearby animal and waited for it to tame. The wolf sniffed at the gift and began to nibble on it, until poof! A red collar appeared around its neck and it barked happily at Chase.

"My turn!" called out Hunter. He did the same thing as Chase, offering another wolf a bone, and soon that one was tamed as well. "I'm going to call you Fang," Hunter decided.

"And you're Tag," Chase told his pet.

Everyone was happy that the skeleton encounter was over and continued on their journey. Hunter and Chase were throwing sticks while their dogs fetched. It was a fun time until they reached a huge mountain and stopped in awe.

"I'm pretty sure this is what we've been looking for," gawked Hunter. In the cliff side was a big cave with a long dark hallway disappearing inside. The opening looked like a gaping mouth with sharp teeth, completed with a nose made from obsidian and eyes glowing with redstone torches. It was terrifying!

"I am NOT going in there," stated Allie. "No way, no how."

"We can't leave you out here," said Red. "What if more skeletons come? Or something worse?"

Allie didn't look convinced.

"Come on, we'll be fine," Hunter pleaded. "We have Fang and Tag now, too. Won't you feel safer if we're all together?"

"I guess," Allie conceded.

The group took out some of their own torches, just in case, and headed into the cave.

CHAPTER 11: HACKER THE MAN

"Do you think he knows we're here?" Roxy whispered to Gil. He only shrugged in response.

It was so quiet, their footsteps were the only thing making sound as they walked down the long tunnel.

"Maybe he's not home," Allie hoped. "This place is giving me the creeps!"

Red looked around in concern. "What's even stranger is that there aren't any mobs around, even though the light level is way below what it takes for them to spawn."

"See?" Allie said. "Even mobs are afraid of him!"

Hunter snorted. "That's silly. Mobs aren't afraid of people."

Allie huffed at his arrogant tone. "Then how do you explain all this Mr. Know It All?"

"Shush, you guys!" Chase exclaimed in a whisper. "You don't want to-"

CLICK.

Everyone froze.

"Run!" shouted Red. The group dashed down the hallway as fast as they could as arrows began to whizz past them from hidden dispensers. They ran until they saw a wall at the end with nowhere else to go, but the moment the friends reached it, the ground suddenly opened up and they fell down into the unknown.

"AAAAAHHHH!"

BUMP.

The friends opened their eyes to find that they were in a huge room of an underground stronghold. Stone bricks, moss, and lava pools made it look old but cool. Except, they realized with horror, that they were standing inside of an

End Portal frame, and on top of a pillar in front of them was a boy with curly blonde hair and an eye of ender in his hands.

"Oh no, not again!" Allie moaned. "I don't want to go to the End!" Roxy took her friend's hand and squeezed it in reassurance.

"Who are you and what are you doing in my house?" asked the stranger.

"Are you Hacker?" asked Hunter.

"Yeah," he responded, "so what?"

Hunter raised his sword. "We're here to put a stop to all the glitching you're doing that's been causing chaos in the world!"

Hacker stood silent for a moment before bursting out in laughter.

"What's so funny?" Hunter asked, his face turning red.

"You think *I'm* the one making a bunch of mobs appear in random places?"

Hunter sword waivered in his hands. Did they have the wrong guy?

"To be fair," Red jumped in, "glitching and hacking are very similar. *And* we were attacked by a horde of skeletons right outside your house."

Hacker frowned. "That's where you're wrong. Hacking is *nothing* like glitching. A glitcher messes with the code. A hacker only accesses it."

The friends exchanged confused glances with each other.

"So you don't actually change anything?" asked Chase.

"Nope."

"Not even to give yourself more stuff?" added Hunter.

"Nope."

"Well that sounds boring," Hunter scoffed.

"Maybe to you," Hacker defended, "but being able to see what everyone in the world is up to is a lot more useful than you can imagine. Plus, I like a challenge. The mods keep putting on new layers of security to prevent me from getting in, but each time I beat them."

"Then why are you in the Griefer Hall of Fame?" wondered Red.

"Is *that* how you found me? I remember getting that invitation a long time ago, but I just threw it away. They figured that since hacking is against the rules, I'm a griefer. No one ever asked me."

"If you're not a griefer, why were you going to send us to the End?" asked Allie.

Hacker put away his eye of ender and pointed down at the portal. "Actually, as you can see, there's no lava under you like there's supposed to be. If I wanted to, I would have just left the lava in there instead of questioning those who come at my door. You never know what kind of people are out there, and anyone brave enough to enter the cave I built would surely be looking for trouble."

"It's definitely scary," Allie agreed.

"And we *did* come here to destroy you," confessed Hunter.

"So if you're not a griefer, would you help us find the ones responsible for all the chaos that's been happening?" asked Roxy.

Hacker thought about it for a moment. "What do I get out of it?"

"Well," said Gil, "you told us you like a challenge, right? The glitcher must be covering his tracks somehow in order to not be banned. That means it would be difficult for you to find him – maybe even impossible."

"Hah! Nothing is impossible for me!" Hacker boasted.

"Then show us," Gil prompted.

"Fine," Hacker agreed, "but you have to make sure you stop that griefer for good. I don't need any trouble at my doorstep."

"It's a deal."

The friends cheered and high fived each other. They climbed out of the portal frame and followed Hacker through the stronghold until they reached a certain room. Inside was a stone platform with a bunch of buttons, switches, and levers.

"Wooah," said Hunter, looking over the mechanical marvel. "What do all these do?"

Hacker went to a chest and took out an iron helmet. Except it definitely wasn't *just* a helmet, because it had what looked like built in sunglasses. Hacker put the helmet on and sat down in front of the switch board.

"Welcome to my control room," he said. "This helmet is my virtual display. From it, I'm able to bypass the graphic interface and get into the code inside."

"That's way better than your black hole," Red told Gil. Gil only shrugged.

Hacker began to push different buttons and levers. The others watched in awe as he worked, waiting to see if he could find the griefer.

"Well this is interesting," Hacker said. "I can trace the code back to a certain location, but it's impossible."

"I thought you said nothing was impossible," Hunter mocked.

Hacker huffed. "I don't mean finding him is impossible. I mean where he's at is impossible."

"And where is that?" asked Red.

"According to the code, the griefer is in the Nether."

Allie gasped. "The Nether? I don't ever want to go back to that place!"

Hunter rolled his eyes. "Oh, it's not *that* bad."

"Did you forget the blazes? And the ghasts? And the-"

"Yeah, yeah." Hunter waved her off.

"But why is it impossible that he's glitching through the Nether?" asked Red.

"Because," Gil went in to explain, "the Nether is a completely different dimension and has a completely separate set of code. There's no way to change stuff here from there."

"But what about when those blazes got sent through?"

Gil shrugged. "Maybe he somehow let one in through a glitched portal and then multiplied it from here. Like I said, there's no way to glitch in the Overworld from the Nether."

"Well, it looks like he found one," Hunter reasoned. "Who knows, maybe he's got a nifty helmet too."

"No way," Hacker argued. "I made mine. And even though I can see the trail going into the Nether, I can't actually get in there myself."

"So what do we do?" asked Roxy.

"I thought it was pretty simple," Hunter replied, drawing his sword. "We're going to the Nether."

"But how do we know where this griefer is?" Allie chimed in. "We can't just walk around yelling 'where are you glitcher?' and expect him to show himself."

"I got something that can help," Hacker said. He went back to his chest and took out another helmet, but this one was golden. "It's a work in progress, but it should do the trick."

"What does it do?" asked Chase.

Hacker smiled proudly. "When you wear it, you can see messed up code. I made it so I could find errors and use them to my advantage."

"Give it to Gil," said Red. "He knows what he's looking at. None of us have any idea what good or bad code looks like."

Hacker nodded and handed the helmet to Gil. "Take care of it," he said. "I want it back when you're done."

Gil nodded and accepted the item. He put it in his inventory for safekeeping and turned to his friends. "I guess we should get going."

"Thanks for everything," Red told Hacker.

"Don't thank me yet," he replied. "And remember your promise."

"One more thing," Hunter added. "Do you have any obsidian by any chance?"

Hacker grinned. "I got something even better."

The gang followed him into another room and gasped. Inside was a Nether portal!

"Wow Hacker, you're the man!" Hunter exclaimed.

Roxy wasn't as thrilled. "Why do you have a Nether portal in your house?" she asked, side-eyeing the boy.

"So I can hack it, of course!"

She shook her head and carefully stepped in along with the others.

"Good luck," Hacker told them as the purple swirls activated. And just like that, he was alone again.

CHAPTER 12: NEVER NETHER

"I *really* hate this place," Gil complained. "It's just too hot."

"I don't mind it," said Red, studying where they popped up. It looked pretty normal as far as the Nether was concerned. Netherrack floor, lavafalls, and a long narrow bridge in the distance leading...somewhere.

"Should we try and get to the bridge? It probably goes into a Nether Fortress," suggested Hunter.

Red shook his head no. "I think it would be better if Gil used the helmet first. Then we'll know which direction we should be heading."

The others agreed and Gil took out the helmet. He put it on and gasped.

"What do you see, Gil?" asked Roxy curiously.

"Everything has a slight green glow to it," Gil described. He kept turning until he suddenly stopped. "There!" He pointed towards the bridge. "Instead of green, the glow is red."

"Are you sure it's not just lava?" Hunter teased.

"I'm sure. There's definitely something there that shouldn't be." He took off the helmet and offered it to Hunter. "Do you want to see?"

Hunter backed away like it was on fire. "No thanks. I'm good."

Gil smirked and put it back in his inventory just in case they were attacked. He didn't want it to get damaged – or worse, broken.

The friends headed towards the bridge while looking out for mobs. They didn't see any, not even zombie pigmen or ghasts. The entire Nether was actually strangely quiet.

Too quiet.

"Something weird is going on here," Roxy whispered to the others. They nodded in agreement. The Nether was never this safe.

"Maybe instead of multiplying the mobs, the griefer accidentally did the opposite," Allie theorized.

"It's possible," Gil admitted. "The Nether code is different from the Overworld's, so he might have gotten confused."

Allie shuddered. "Having no mobs is even creepier than having a bunch of them."

The others agreed.

They reached the bridge with no problems and saw that at the end of it was a door leading inside a wall of nether brick.

Hunter grinned. "I told you guys! It's a Nether Fortress!"

"We're not here for treasure," Red reminded him. "We're here to stop a griefer."

"I know, I know," Hunter grumbled, "but that doesn't mean we can't get treasure if we see some."

Red shook his head and led the others to the door. The bridge went high up in the air, with a river of lava boiling below them. The friends huddled close together, keeping away from the edges. Falling would mean certain death.

CLICK.

Red froze. They were halfway in, with a long way both in front and behind them.

"Um…what was that?" squeaked Allie.

She didn't have to wait for an answer. The door of the Nether Fortress opened and angry mobs began to pour out. Ghasts, blazes, enraged zombie pigmen – everything that the Nether could spawn, was locked away behind that one door.

"RUN!" yelled Red, but the moment they turned around, an explosion rocked the bridge. Whatever mechanism opened the door also ignited a block of TNT – right behind the gang. The bridge went up in flames, leaving a hole that led straight down into lava.

The mobs were getting closer with each passing moment.

"What do we do?" cried Roxy.

Hunter raised his sword. "We have to fight!"

The others drew their weapons and prepared for the battle of a lifetime. Red and Gil slashed with their diamond swords. Hunter and Chase used their enchanted golden ones. Roxy and Allie fired their bows at the flying mobs. Even Fang and Tag were attacking some wither skeletons.

"Ouch!" Allie screamed as a fireball hit her. "There's just too many of them!"

Red hated to admit it, but she was right. They could hold down the bridge for a while, but they couldn't stand there forever. Eventually, their armor and weapons would break.

"I have a plan," Gil called out, "here, take my stuff."

Red reluctantly accepted Gil's items as he immediately knew what Gil wanted to do. "But I thought you said you can't glitch in the Nether, Gil?"

Gil smiled back at his friend. "Don't worry about it. All you need to do is survive just a little longer."

Red nodded, and with a farewell wave of his hand, Gil jumped over the ledge and disappeared into the lava.

"Gil!" Roxy yelled after him.

"It's ok, Roxy," Red reassured her. "We have to trust him."

"We don't have a choice," Chase added as he swung again, destroying a zombie pigman. With each fallen mob, another came. More and more were spilling out of the fortress, forcing the friends back to the edge of the bridge where the blast broke it apart.

"Oh Gil," Roxy begged, "hurry!"

Just in that moment, something began to materialize out of thin air around them. They moved out of its way, driving the mobs forward with one big push.

"It's a Nether portal!" squealed Allie. With relief, they saw that she was right. A frame of obsidian appeared before them, the purple swirls inviting instead of menacing for a change.

"Let's go!" charged Hunter. The girls jumped in first, followed by the boys and their dogs. Just as three fireballs made their way towards them, the friends vanished out of the Nether – and back to the Overworld.

CHAPTER 13: A SNOWY SURPRISE

CRUNCH!

"Oh no!" Allie moaned. "Anywhere but here!"

The group found themselves knee-deep in snow next to a Nether portal. Around them were some scattered spruce trees covered in snow, and what looked like a frozen river ahead.

"Brrrr." Roxy shivered. "And I thought the taiga was bad! This is a million times colder!"

"After the Nether, I don't mind a little fresh air," Hunter said. "But we should probably go get Gil."

"Yes," agreed Chase, "I want to thank him for getting us out of there in one piece."

"First, we need to find a village. It's getting late," Red remarked. "Once we eat and get some rest, we'll go to Gil's house."

"Do you know where one is?" asked Allie.

Red gave her a hopeful smile. "Usually, if we follow a river, we can find one."

They began to trudge through the snow. It was so thick, they couldn't see their feet! After a little while, they couldn't *feel* them, either. The only ones who didn't seem affected by the cold were Fang and Tag. Hunter began to make snowballs and throw them for the dogs to catch. Allie and Roxy climbed on to the frozen river and glided on the slippery ice. It was actually pretty fun!

However, the day was at its end, and they began to feel nervous. Luckily, Red was right, and soon they saw torches gleaming in the setting sun. A village! Wood and stone houses topped with snow stood in the distance.

"Last one there is a rotten zombie!" called out Hunter.

"You're on!" Roxy accepted.

The friends used their remaining energy and sprinted towards it. They entered the gates just in time. Mobs began to spawn on the outskirts, staying away from the bright torches that lined the fence.

"Look!" Allie pointed. "It's a snow golem!"

A snowman-like creature with a pumpkin head was heading towards them.

"I've never seen one of those before," Roxy marveled.

"There's another one! And another!"

The group looked around to see that several snow golems were now slowly coming at them.

"What are they doing?" asked Chase.

"I don't know, but I don't like it," replied Hunter.

Red's forehead furrowed. "Snow golems are utility mobs. They're supposed to protect us from hostiles."

The first golem finally stopped a small distance ahead.

THUMP!

"Ouch!" cried Roxy. "It threw a snowball at me!"

THUMP!

"GURGLRGLR!" Hunter sputtered as a snowball hit him straight in the face.

"They're attacking us!" Red realized.

Chase deflected a snowball with his sword. "But why?"

"It must be the griefer's work!" Hunter bellowed. He raised his weapon at the golem, but Red yelled at him to stop.

"These snow golems aren't doing any damage. There's no reason to destroy them. Let's just find shelter and hide out until morning. Maybe Gil will figure out a way to fix them by then."

Tired and weak, Hunter agreed. The friends ran to the nearest large house and knocked on the door. A villager opened it and let them in.

"Thank you," Allie told him as the door shut behind them.

"Are those snow golems acting up again?" the villager asked.

Red nodded. "They're shooting snow balls at us. Has it happened before?"

The villager shook his head up and down. "Oh yes, they've been doing it randomly for days now. We don't know how to make them stop. It's not terribly bothersome, but it's definitely strange."

"I love it!" a little baby villager exclaimed from behind his dad. "I can have a snow ball fight with them!"

"Go to bed, son," the villager told him sternly. "It's past your bedtime."

The baby villager pouted but listened.

"At least they're not hurting anyone," Red said, watching the baby run off upstairs.

The villager offered the friends some mushroom soup, and they happily ate it. Once full, they retreated to his guest room and even though he had to make a few extra beds, there was enough room for everyone to sleep. Red hoped that Gil was watching over them and would fix the golems, but even if he wasn't, they would make sure to tell him when they got to his house. And with those thoughts, he finally drifted off to sleep.

CHAPTER 14: A STICKY SWAMP

In the morning, the gang had some breakfast and headed outside. They saw the snow golems walking around, but they didn't seem hostile.

"Look!" said Roxy. She was pointing at a wooden sign right next to the villager's house. It read 'Golems fixed. Nether = trap. Hurry. – Gil'.

"He did it!" Allie cheered. "He un-glitched the golems!"

"But what did he mean by the Nether being a trap?" wondered Chase. "And did Hacker know about it?"

Hunter growled in anger. "I bet he did! I bet he was a griefer all along and sent us there on purpose!"

"Let's not jump to conclusions," Red reasoned. "How about we get to Gil, first. I'm sure he'll have all the answers."

They thanked the villager for his hospitality and went on their way. Looking at the map, to get to the forest biome, they had to cross a swamp.

"Swamps are icky," shuddered Allie. "And they have witches."

"I'll protect you," Hunter boasted. "No ugly wart-nosed witch is going to get through me!"

Roxy rolled her eyes. Hunter was always way overconfident.

Soon, the snow returned to grass, and spruce trees became replaced with oaks. The temperature warmed up and the friends relaxed. Hunter and Chase were busy playing with their dogs when they reached the dreaded swamp.

The swampland looked darker than normal forest biomes, even in the middle of the day. The ground felt mushy. Shallow murky waters sported floating lily pads, and trees had dark green vines growing from them. Mushrooms and sugarcane popped up here and there.

Roxy peered into the brackish green liquid. "Eeew," she said with a grimace. "Water is *not* supposed to look like *that*."

They walked carefully, just wanting to get through as fast as possible.

WOOOSH!

Rain came out of nowhere! Immediately, the friends were soaked and unable to figure out which way to go.

"There!" yelled out Chase, pointing in the distance. "There's a house!"

Without a second thought, everyone dashed to the looming structure ahead. But the moment they reached it, they stopped in their tracks.

"It's a witch hut!" exclaimed Allie.

Hunter drew his sword. "I'll take care of it!" He pushed open the door and ran inside. The others followed, afraid of what they might see.

Upon entering, they sagged with relief. The hut was empty. They could wait out the rain and continue on after.

The interior was made from oak logs and spruce planks. There was a crafting table and cauldron, along with a mushroom flower pot. The cauldron was filled with a bubbling green liquid.

Hunter studied the concoction. "I wonder what it is."

"Probably a potion of some kind," Red guessed.

"Why don't you try it and find out?" Roxy dared.

"Why don't *you*?" countered Hunter.

"No thanks. I don't want to grow a second head or something."

Allie giggled and the others laughed. They sat down and had a snack while the rain pounded at the roof of the hut.

"Ruff! Ruff!" Fang barked at the door. The group froze.

"Ruff!" Tag joined his canine companion.

"Do you think the witch came back?" Allie whispered. No one knew, so they sat quietly, holding their breath while trying to listen through the rain.

Suddenly, a vial flew in the side window and shattered on the floor! A green mist came out of it, and shrouded the friends in its effect.

"Oh no!" cried Roxy. "We've been poisoned!"

"Quickly," Red said, handing out milk from his inventory, "drink this before-"

Another potion was thrown inside, and this time, black swirls filled the air.

"It's a potion of weakness," Chase realized.

"We have to get outside and destroy the witch before she throws some harming potions in here," urged Red.

Hunter was first out the door, followed by Chase and Red. Allie and Roxy stayed back, drawing their arrows.

The witch had on a black hat and dark purple robes. Her huge nose twitched when she saw her attackers, and she cackled.

"Watch out!" Red yelled to Hunter, but it was too late. Hunter lunged at the woman, and was soaked in a potion of slowness. His speed dropped and the witch quickly moved out of the way.

THWACK. THWACK.

Two arrows lodged themselves in her, taking down a little bit of health. The potion of weakness dramatically decreased their strength. The only way to defeat the witch was for everyone to attack together.

And that's exactly what they did. Red slashed with his diamond sword, while Chase and Hunter hit her from behind. Roxy and Allie fired more arrows. The witch tried to drink a healing potion, but it wasn't enough. The friends were too much for her, even with all her stat reducing tricks.

Finally, the mob was destroyed! Everyone cheered and high fived each other. They drank some more milk to regain their strength, and by the time they were done, so was the rain.

Determined to make the journey before nightfall, they headed out to the forest biome. It was time to go see Gil and get some answers.

CHAPTER 15: A TRICKY TRAP

Gil waved at his friends as they walked up to his house. "Hey everyone!"

He invited them inside and offered some cake, which they were happy to accept. While eating, they told Gil about their adventures in the snow and swamp biomes.

"I wish I was there to help you guys," Gil said after they were done.

"You saved all our lives in the Nether," Red reminded him. "Speaking of which, how *did* you do that? I thought you couldn't glitch in the Nether from the Overworld?"

Gil smiled. "That's true, but the portals between the dimensions are connected. You only need to build one for it to appear in the other. All I had to do was use the coordinates of where I destroyed, and make the adjoining portal in the Overworld to link with them. I adjusted a little for height, of course, but overall it was pretty easy."

"Wow," admired Allie. "You're really smart, Gil."

Gil blushed. "Thanks."

"Now that that's figured out, tell us about this trap," Hunter insisted. "Did Hacker send us to be destroyed?"

Gil shook his head no. "Actually, it was Hacker who told me what it was. He sent me a message through the code. Apparently, he was looking into the Nether portal some more, and realized that the trail he saw going in from the griefer was a fake. He couldn't tell why, but he knew it must have been a trap to lure anyone wanting to seek out the griefer. He immediately tried to contact me and saw that he was right. We were tricked."

"I still don't trust him," Hunter huffed. "I think he's just covering for himself."

"If he was," Gil continued, "would he have given us the griefer's *true* identity?"

Everyone gasped.

"You know who it is?" asked Roxy.

"I sure do," Gil said with a grin. "Hacker was so angry he was tricked, that he put all his brainpower into getting answers. I helped sift through the code until we found the real trail."

"Where did it lead you?" asked Allie.

"To Mushroom Island."

"Ooh! I've always wanted to visit a mushroom biome!"

Gil smiled. "Well, you'll get the chance to now."

"That still doesn't answer *who* the griefer is," Hunter argued.

"Actually, it does," Red commented. "The only griefer I remember being from the Mushroom Biome is Modder. He creates all kinds of mods so he can cheat. I wouldn't put it past him to use a breach for dealing chaos to the world."

Hunted stood up. "I'm ready to take him out. Who's with me?"

"I think I'll stay," said Gil. "I'll probably just end up needing to come back anyway."

"Not this again," groaned Hunter.

Red turned to his friend. "Would you be able to close the breach from here?"

Gil thought about the question. "I don't know. I would have to see it to know what to do."

"Then you have to come or the entire trip would be a waste."

Gil nodded. Red was right. Without him, they wouldn't be able to stop the griefer for good. He was coming, whether he liked it or not.

"Well, it's getting pretty late since it took you guys a while to get here with the witch altercation. How about you spend the night and we'll tackle this griefer in the morning?"

The sun was setting but the friends were way too excited to sleep. Instead, Gil took them down to his basement and showed them the breach. No one wanted to even touch it, which made Gil laugh. It wasn't *that* scary, he thought.

"AAH! HELP!" a scream came from outside. The gang rushed out of the house to see what was going on. An enderman was attacking a villager! Hunter and Red ran up and quickly destroyed it with their swords.

"You're ok now," Red told the terrified villager.

"Thank you," the man replied. "I saw the enderman right outside and accidentally looked it in the eyes. I didn't mean to, it just happened so fast!"

"It's alright," Red assured him. The villager scrambled home while Hunter and Red joined the others.

"What's an enderman doing here?" wondered Gil. "They usually don't come around these parts."

The night was now in full swing, and they looked around to see if they could spot anything strange.

"Uh oh," said Roxy. "I think I figured out where the enderman came from." She pointed ahead.

Right beyond the torch-lit gate was a row of endermen, their purple eyes gleaming in the darkness. But what was even worse, was the Ender portal behind them, from which more endermen poured out with every passing moment.

"Wha...how is this possible?" Hunter muttered.

"It must be the griefer," Red guessed. "We have to get to that Ender portal and destroy it before the entire village is overrun."

"Does anyone have any pumpkins?" asked Gil.

"I have a few," Red replied, looking in his inventory.

"We'll go and take care of the portal." Hunter and Chase volunteered. Red handed them the pumpkins and they put them on like helmets.

"Be careful," Red warned them. "We don't know if these endermen act normal, or if they've been glitched. Stand back to back so if one aggros and teleports behind you, you can still block its attack."

It was a good idea. The two side-stepped awkwardly down to the portal, while Red and the girls defended other villagers who accidentally aggroed the mobs. There were just too many endermen to not be able to look one in the eye. Gil went back to his house so he could jump in the breach and see if he could help.

"Just a little further," Hunter grunted as they neared the portal. Walking sideways was very uncomfortable, especially when you're wading through a sea of tall black mobs. They almost reached it when they heard a familiar growl coming from inside, followed by a loud flapping of giant wings.

"It's the ender dragon!" cried Hunter. He jumped back in fright – and right into an enderman! The enderman became enraged and attacked. Hunter defended, but the moment he went to swing at the mob, it vanished.

"Watch out," Hunter warned his friend. The enderman reappeared right in front of Chase, ready to strike. It was met with a sword, and was quickly destroyed.

ROAR!

The ground began to shake as a dark shadow emerged from the portal.

"We have to stop it, right now!" Hunter dashed for the frame, not caring if he bumped into endermen along the way, and hit it as hard as he could. The block shattered, and the portal flickered. The dragon bellowed in anger, but it couldn't get through anymore, and with one last growl it seceded back to the End just as the portal deactivated.

Hunter and Chase cheered, but it wasn't time to celebrate just yet. There were a ton of angry endermen ready to strike after Hunter's heroic leap. The friends fought hard, but there were just too many.

WOOOSH!

Rain fell down from the sky! The endermen screamed and began to teleport away, damaged by the water.

"Alright Gil!"

Everyone was glad to be rid of the mobs and retreated to the safety and warmth of the house. Gil joined them a moment later, happy to have helped. This time, they were definitely tired and quickly went to sleep, dreaming about finding Modder and stopping him for good.

CHAPTER 16: THE MUSHROOM MEETING

Inventory stocked, gear repaired, and health bars full, the friends felt ready to take on anyone. They headed out to the mushroom biome. Since it was an island, they crafted three boats: one for Red and Gil, another for Hunter and Chase, and a third for Roxy and Allie. They also had some spare ones just in case. All the pets stayed at Gil's house to be safe.

The boats glided across the water, bringing the crew closer and closer to their destination. Soon, they were able to see a big island with purple-tinted ground made from mycelium, a fungus-type block. Huge mushrooms with red and brown tops were scattered around like trees. The terrain was pretty open and flat, with one big hill in the middle.

The boats came to shore, letting out their riders.

"This is amazing," marveled Roxy. "And look!" She pointed ahead. "A mooshroom!"

The others turned and saw a red and white spotted cow with mushrooms growing on its back.

"Mooshrooms are pretty cool," said Red. "They can be sheared, milked, and make mushroom stew. If I could take one home, I would."

"We're not here for the cows," Hunter pressed. "I want to go find the griefer!"

Gil took out the helmet that Hacker gave him and put it on. He slowly looked around and stopped at the right side of the hill. "There." He pointed to a small cave.

106

"Are you sure Hacker isn't trying to mess with us?" Hunter asked one last time. "He hasn't exactly proven himself trustworthy."

"I'm sure," Gil replied. "I was there when we looked for the griefer. He taught me a lot of things about how to navigate the code to find what I'm looking for. Plus, we know where he lives."

Hunter's face widened with a smile. "That's true. If he *is* lying, he's next on the list."

They made their way to the cave, passing all kinds of small mushrooms. They reached the opening and saw a dark tunnel going inside.

"What if there are mobs in there?" Allie asked.

"Don't worry," Red told her, "hostile mobs don't spawn on this island, even at night."

Her mouth fell open. "Really? We should come live here!"

"It's true," Gil confirmed. "This is the safest place in the whole world."

They lit some torches so they could see and entered the darkness. It wasn't long before they heard something in front of them.

BUUH.

"Eeek!" Allie squeaked. "I thought you guys said there weren't any hostile mobs?"

Hunter charged at the zombie and quickly destroyed it. "I guess we didn't account for the griefer's messing around."

BUUUH. BUUUUH.

"There's more coming," Red warned. "Get ready."

The friends put their torches on the walls and prepared for battle. Zombies came at them like a scene from a horror movie. They moaned and groaned, reaching for anyone they could get to before being struck down by swords and flaming arrows. It wasn't long before every mob was destroyed and the path was clear.

"This griefer is running out of tricks," mocked Hunter. "Let's get him!"

He dashed down the hallway, leaving the others running after him.

"Hunter! Wait!" Roxy yelled, but he didn't stop.

Suddenly, a bright light appeared at the end. They entered it and saw that they were in a huge dome chamber filled with treasure chests. At the center stood a throne made from gold on a diamond pedestal. In that throne sat none other

108

than Modder. He wore a royal robe of embroidered emeralds and a golden crown on his head. In his hands was a golden scepter with a red ornament at the top. He looked like a king.

"Welcome to my home," Modder told his visitors. "You have proven to be quite the adversaries."

"And YOU have proven to be quite a pain in my butt," Hunter replied. "Now surrender or-"

Modder bellowed out in laughter. "Or what? You and your little friends will try to poke me with your shabby swords and meager arrows?"

Roxy raised an eyebrow. "Why is he talking like that?" she whispered.

Chase shrugged. "Maybe he really thinks he's some kind of a king and is trying to stay in character."

Not wasting any time, Hunter raised his sword but was interrupted by an unfamiliar voice.

"I wouldn't do that if I were you."

Everyone looked over to the left and saw another person there, standing on top of a treasure chest. It was a boy in a checkered suit with orange hair.

"The Multiplier!" exclaimed Gil.

The others turned to him. "Another griefer?" whimpered Allie.

"That's right," Multi said. "Did you really think all those mobs multiplied themselves?"

"Who do you think gave Multi his multiplying mod?" Modder explained. "We've been working together this whole time. Ever since I found the code breach, we've been putting a ton of mobs where they don't belong, and even messing around with existing ones. Every day we learn something new, and soon no one will be able to stand in our way."

Roxy turned to Gil. "We have to stop him. Can you find the breach?"

Gil nodded. It had to be in one of the chests. He reached in his inventory for Hacker's helmet, except...

"The helmet! It's gone!"

"Looking for this?" a female voice behind them asked. They whirled around to see a girl with pink armor and pink hair holding Hacker's helmet in her hands.

"Swiper? You're in on this too?" Gil gaped in shock.

"Of course," Swiper replied. "What better way to steal stuff if not in the middle of chaos?"

"Give it back," Gil told her, but she only laughed.

"So you can find and close the breach? No thanks. I like things just the way they are."

"Then we'll have to *get* it back," Gil warned. He drew his sword and moved to Swiper.

"One more step and the ground under you will be nothing but an empty crater."

The friends gasped. Blaster was standing on top of a chest to their right, holding a block of TNT.

"You!" Hunter exclaimed. "What are *you* doing here? Didn't Swiper steal your stuff?"

He snorted. "I found her and got it back. And then she told me about this awesome griefer alliance and I decided I would join in the fun. Did you like all those creepers we sent to your house?"

Hunter only growled in response.

"This is not good," said Roxy.

"It's still six against four," Red told her. "We got this."

And then he heard a CLICK and the floor began to move under their feet.

"What's going on?" Allie cried out, grabbing Chase's arm to steady herself. Blocks shifted around, crumbling at the edges and leaving a gaping hole. The friends huddled close together as the floor fell away and became a small platform.

"Even if you destroy us," Hunter yelled to Modder, "we'll be back, and we'll get you."

Modder smirked. "Oh, I don't plan on destroying you. I plan on something much, much worse."

The friends glanced over at each other in confusion. What could possibly be worse?

"Bye bye." Modder waved. "See you never."

The rest of the ground fell away, taking its occupants down into nothingness.

CHAPTER 17: AVOIDING THE VOID

Bonk.

The friends fell right on top of a stone platform. It was a perfect square, with nothing on it except a single block of cobblestone at the center.

They looked around in awe. The sky was completely black. Actually, everything was black. Red peeked over the edge of the platform to find that there was nothing beyond but more blackness. The ground itself was only one block thick.

"What is this place?" asked Roxy.

"It's The Void," answered Gil.

"What's The Void?" asked Allie.

"The Void is a special biome that can't be accessed without a customized setting," Gil explained. "Basically, no one can get in – or out."

"We could jump off," proposed Red.

Gil nodded and handed Red his items. "Good idea. Once I'm home, I can get all of you guys out of here too."

Everyone waved bye to Gil as he went over to the edge. He took a deep breath and jumped off.

And respawned right back in the middle of the platform.

"Ummm…what just happened?" asked Hunter.

Gil shook his head in confusion. "I don't understand. Modder must have messed with the code and made it impossible for us to return to our original spawn point."

Roxy's eyes widened. "Are you saying that we're trapped here…forever?"

Gil didn't respond. Everyone stood in silence, trying to think of a way out, but no one had any ideas.

Just then, a bright blue beam shot up in the air out of the cobblestone block. The friends jumped back in surprise, staring at the new development.

"Now what?" moaned Allie. "How much worse could this get?"

"That depends," a booming voice perforated the air, "do you want to sit around here twiddling your thumbs, or do you want to go kick some griefer butt?"

"Hacker!" Gil exclaimed. "How did you find us?"

Hacker's voice laughed from the beam of light. "I figured you guys would probably need my help since you can't glitch," he explained, "so I've been following your moves through my helmet and saw what happened."

"It's a good thing you did," Red said, "or we'd be stuck here for good."

"So how do we get out?" asked Hunter eagerly.

"Just touch the beam and you'll be teleported back to the same place you were when you fell.

Don't worry, they've already repaired the floor so you won't fall again. They think they've won."

"And we're about to prove them wrong," Hunter cackled.

"Thank you, Hacker," said Red. "I know you don't like changing the code. We appreciate you breaking your own rules to save us."

"It's no big deal. Now get out there and get those griefers."

"One more thing," Gil said before touching the beam, "do you know where the breach is in the room? Swiper stole the helmet you gave me so I haven't been able to find it in time."

"No," Hacker replied, "you'll just have to do it the old fashioned way and open each chest. Then, when you find it, just destroy the chest and the breach will be closed with it."

Gil nodded. "Got it. Thanks again!"

The group surrounded the beam and all touched it at the same time. Their bodies turned to pure light as they teleported, happily leaving The Void and coming back to the Overworld.

CHAPTER 18: A VALIANT VICTORY

They opened their eyes just to find themselves face-to-face with the four griefers high-fiving each other at the throne. The griefers' expressions transformed into shock as they saw the friends materialize out of thin air.

"What? How did you escape from The Void?" sputtered Modder. "It's impossible!"

"Nothing is impossible," said Hunter, repeating Hacker's words, "and now you're going to pay." He raised his sword and charged at the king-wannabe.

Swiper, Blaster, and Multi rolled out of the way as Hunter's weapon sliced at empty space. He blinked in disbelief and looked up in the air to where he just saw Modder *fly* to. The griefer hovered in place like he had wings, but none were visible.

"Hah!" he laughed. "You really think you can defeat me and my mods?"

Hunger growled in frustration. An arrow whizzed by his head at hit Modder right in the chest! The griefer looked down at it sticking out of his robes and laughed even harder.

"I told you, I'm invincible! There's nothing you can do to stop me!" He turned to his colleagues. "Now get them!"

Blaster took out a block of TNT in each hand and grinned. "Let's play." He lit them and threw one at Hunter and the other to the rest of the group. They all jumped out just in time, the explosions shaking the dome.

Roxy and Allie drew their enchanted arrows and began to fire as Multiplier and Blaster engaged in a battle with Hunter and Chase. Modder must have given his minions some kind of special mods because their health was higher than any person's they'd ever seen. The friends would have to give it their all to defeat the griefers.

Meanwhile, Red and Gil ran over to the chests and began to open them, one by one, looking for the breach. They were all filled with stolen treasures – diamonds, emeralds, gold, you name it!

"Look out!" Red yelled to Gil as he watched Swiper appear behind him with a swirling purple sword. Gil turned and blocked her attack with his own weapon. Surprised, she jumped back.

"You don't have to do this, Swiper," he told her. "You can stop being a griefer and make real friends, ones who would appreciate you, not make you fight their battles for them."

"No way, Glitcher," Swiper replied. "I like stealing. It's what I was spawned to do, just like you were made for glitching. Come back to us and we'll forgive you for this little transgression. We're your real friends, not these losers."

Gil felt a flame of anger ignite inside his chest. "Don't call my friends losers," he said in a menacing tone. Swiper backed up, feeling uneasy by his sudden change of demeanor. He might have given up being a griefer, but Gil's reputation was there for a reason.

"Last chance," he told Swiper, "or I'll make sure you end up exactly where you belong."

He saw Swiper hesitate, and then something unexpected happened. She dropped her sword and sprinted away through the tunnel as fast as her legs could carry her. Gil grinned at the fleeing girl, filling with pride.

"Come back here, you coward!" Modder yelled after Swiper. "ARGH!"

He turned towards Gil and focused his eyes on the ex-griefer. "You'll pay for that!"

"You don't care about Swiper! You only kept her around to steal stuff for you," Gil accused him. Modder's face turned red like it was going to explode, and then...

Two laser beams shot out of his eyes and straight at Gil!

"Ouch!" Gil cried out as he was hit head on. He was thrown back from the force, dropping his sword. He looked down to see that his armor broke, leaving him defenseless. Modder laughed maniacally and prepared another blast. Gil shielded his face, unable to protect himself any other way, when he saw Red step right in front of him and block the laser with his diamond sword.

"Go! Go!" Red urged. "I can't hold him here forever. Find that breach!"

Gil nodded and even though he didn't want to leave his friend, he knew their best chance of winning was to get ahold of that breach. He quickly searched one chest after another, hoping he would find the right one before Red was overpowered.

CLANK!

He turned in horror to see Red's sword snap in half. The force of the laser sent Red flying across the room. He hit the wall and collapsed limply on the floor.

"RED!" cried Gil after his friend.

"You're next," Modder told him.

At that moment, Hunter blocked Modder's line of sight with his own body. "You'll have to go through me, first."

Modder sneered. "With pleasure." The lasers shot out again, this time hitting Hunter's weapon, slowly destroying it. Gil didn't waste any time. He kept looking, until finally he saw the familiar black hole.

"I got it!" he shouted with joy. But when he looked up, he saw Hunter fall to the ground, his sword disintegrated. Without a second thought, Gil jumped into the breach.

"NOO!" yelled Modder, but it was too late.

The remaining friends watched with bated breath as Modder's lasers vanished and he dropped to the floor, his flying abilities gone. He scrambled to his feet, furious at the loss of his powers.

"What the..." Blaster mumbled as all the TNT in his hands and inventory transformed into blocks of dirt.

"It's...it's the Glitcher!" stammered Multi.

"Yay! Go Gil!" cheered Roxy and Allie.

A dark swirling abyss began to form at the center of the room. Everyone moved away from it, afraid of where it might lead.

"Aaaah!" Modder yelled, and the friends saw that he was getting sucked into the dark portal.

"Noo! Help us!" Blaster and Multi were also being dragged in! The others watched as the three griefers tried crawling away to no avail. The pull was too strong, and with one last scream they disappeared inside. The portal swooshed and vanished, leaving nothing but the floor beneath.

CHAPTER 19: A FINAL MISSION

"Where did they go?" wondered Roxy.

"I think that's something we'll have to ask Gil when he comes back," said Chase.

"Oh no! Hunter!" cried Allie, spying her friend. She ran to him, while Roxy went to Red. They were relieved to see that both were alive, though barely. It took everyone's potions of healing to get them back on their feet.

"Where's Gil?" asked Red, looking around for his friend.

"He hasn't returned yet," Roxy replied, "but I'm sure he'll be back soon."

As if he heard her, Gil finally appeared out of the chest.

"Hey guys." He smiled. "I'm glad to see everyone's ok."

"Thanks to you," said Red.

Gil shook his head. "Without you, I wouldn't have been able to get to the breach and stop them in time."

"Let's call it a team effort," Hunter suggested. The group agreed.

"Where did you send the griefers?" asked Roxy curiously.

Gil grinned. "Exactly where they sent us."

Allie gasped. "You mean to The Void?"

He nodded. "It was the only place I could be sure they'd be harmless."

"You don't think that's kind of...mean?" asked Chase.

Gil shrugged. "I left them a bunch of materials so they can make more land and grow stuff. I'll check in every once in a while and see how they're doing. Maybe they'll have a change of heart and decide to become good and I'll let them out. Or maybe not."

Hunter leaned over to Chase and whispered, "Remind me never to get on Gil's bad side, ok?"

Chase nodded in agreement.

"What should we do now?" asked Hunter, trying to change the subject. "I mean look at all these chests! There's got to be a fortune in here!"

"There's one thing I have to do first." Gil walked over to the breach and struck the chest as hard as he could. It shattered, destroying the breach along with it.

"Good riddance," said Roxy.

"You know what would be a good idea?" proposed Allie. "We can take all the treasures we find here and give them out to all the villages that Modder and his crew destroyed."

"That's a great idea!" exclaimed Roxy.

Everyone except Hunter agreed.

"Don't we deserve to keep some of it?" he argued.

"It's not ours to take," Red reasoned. "It belongs to the people they stole from. And since we can't know who exactly, we'll just have to share with everyone."

Hunter rolled his eyes. "Fine."

"Don't worry, Hunter," Roxy told him, "once you see all those villagers praising your name for bringing them all these diamonds, you'll be feeling much better."

Hunter's face lit up. "I'll be hailed a hero! Savior of the world!"

Everyone laughed. "You keep thinking that."

They began to collect the items from the chests, and soon their inventories were full. They would have to come back several times to clean out all of it.

With one final look around the cavern, the friends left on a new journey – to right Modder's wrongs and bring peace and happiness back to the Overworld.

At least until nightfall.

The End